LEF

THE SEVEN DAYS OF CREATION

adapted from the Bible and illustrated by

LEONARD EVERETT FISHER

Holiday House, New York

Library of Congress Cataloging in Publication Data

Fisher, Leonard Everett.
The seven days of creation

Summary: Brief text and illustrations retell the story of the Creation.
1. Creation—Juvenile literature. [1. Creation. 2. Bible stories—O.T.] I. Title.
BS651.F53 222'.1109505 81-2952
ISBN 0-8234-0398-X AACR2

Once there was a watery vastness without life or light.
Only the spirit of God moved across the darkness.

Then God said, "Let there be light."
And there was light.
God called the light Day.
And the darkness, He called Night.
This was the end of the first day.

On the second day, God divided the vastness
above and below.

He called the upper part Heaven.

On the third day, God gathered the waters below and allowed the seas and dry land to appear.

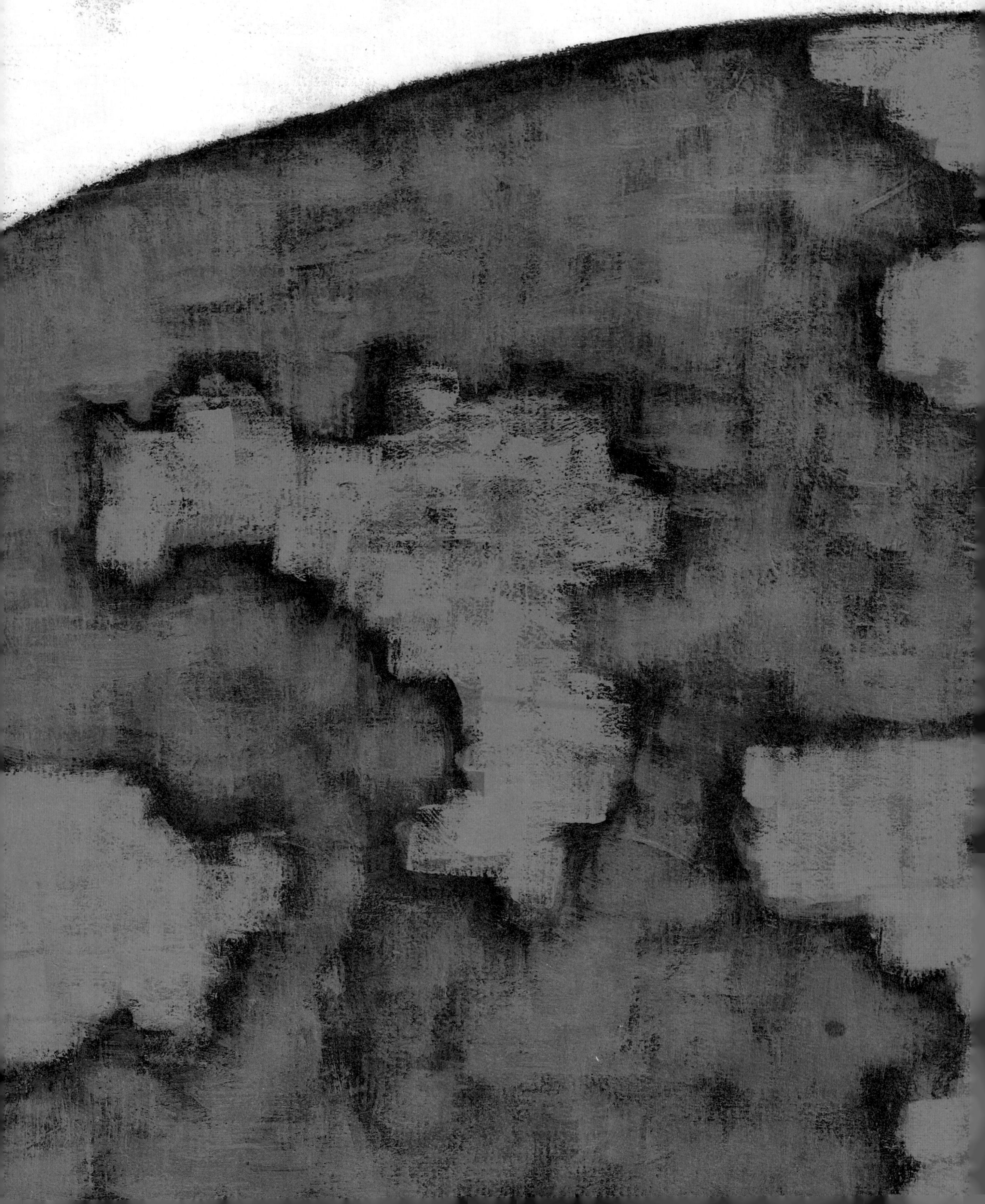

He called this Earth.

Then God said, "Let there be grass and flowers and trees on Earth." And it was so.

On the fourth day, God created the sun
to shine upon Earth.

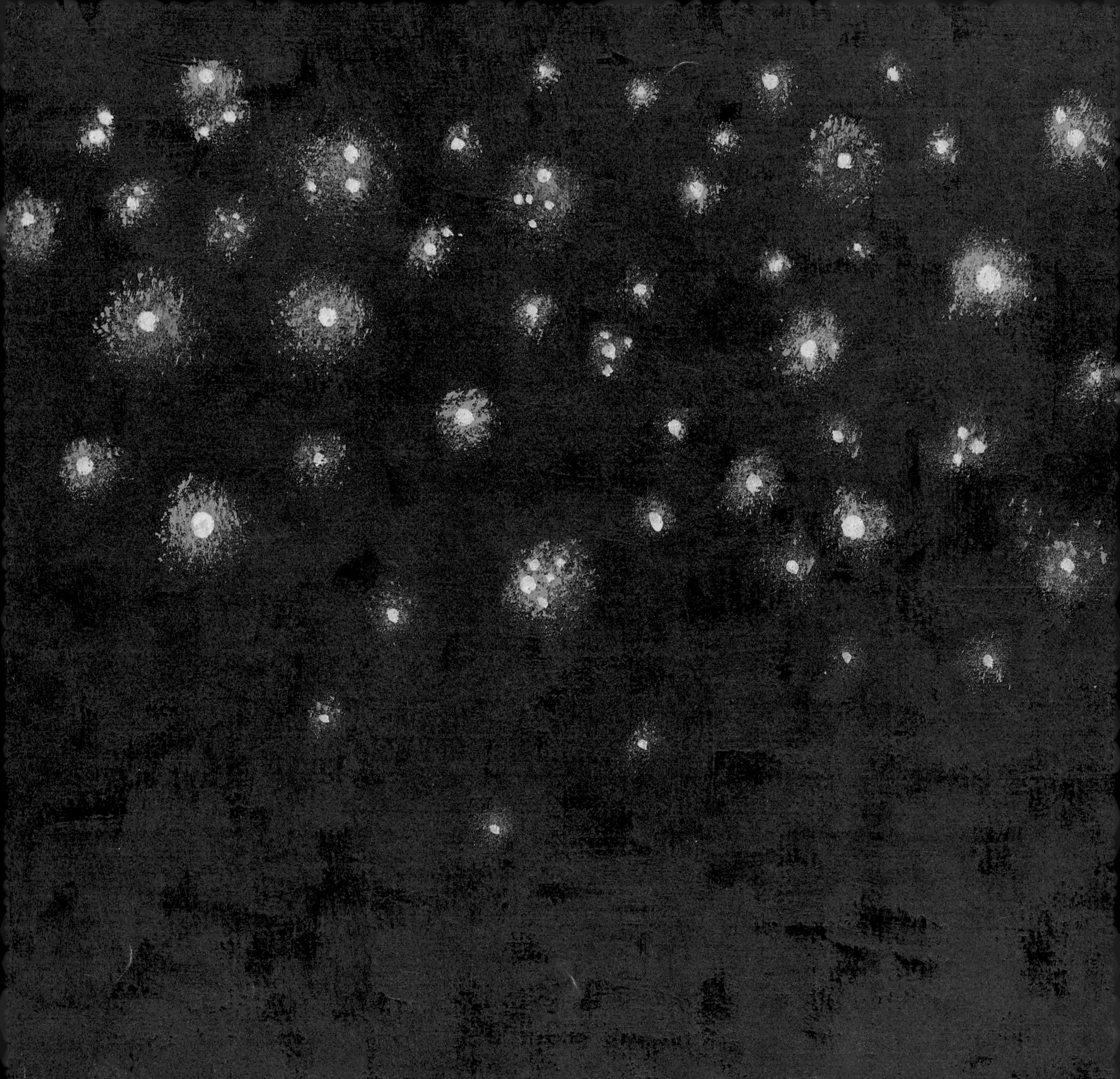

And He made the moon and stars to shine upon Earth too.
This was the end of the fourth day.

On the fifth day, God made fish to swim in the seas . . .

and birds to fly in the air.

On the sixth day, God made animals
to roam the dry land.

Then God created man to rule over every creature
that swam in the seas; that flew in the air;
that roamed the dry land.

But God did not want man to be alone.
So He created woman.
And this was the end of the sixth day.

Now it was the seventh day. God's work was finished.
He saw that it was good, and He rested.

This book was set in Perpetua and Weiss types by Hallmark Press, Inc.
It was printed by offset on 80-lb. Moistrite Matte by Rae Publishing Co.
and bound by The Book Press.
The art was produced with acrylic paints.
Color separations were made by Capper, Inc.